P9-BIA-672

DO YOU ENJOY BEING FRIGHTENED?

WOULD YOU RATHER HAVE
NIGHTMARES
INSTEAD OF SWEET DREAMS?

ARE YOU HAPPY ONLY WHEN
SHAKING WITH FEAR?

CONGRATULATIONS ! ! ! !

YOU'VE MADE A WISE CHOICE.

THIS BOOK IS THE DOORWAY
TO ALL THAT MAY FRIGHTEN YOU.

GET READY FOR

COLD, CLAMMY SHIVERS
RUNNING UP AND DOWN YOUR SPINE!

NOW, OPEN THE DOOR–
IF YOU DARE !!!!

Shivers™

THE TERRIBLE TERROR BOOK

M. D. Spenser

This book may not be reproduced in whole or in
part, or stored in any type of retrieval system, or
transmitted in any way or via any means electronic,
mechanical, photocopying, or recording without
permission of the publisher.

Copyright © 1998 by M.D. Spenser. All rights
reserved.

Published by Peter Haddock Ltd., England, by
arrangement with River Publishing, Inc. All right,
title and interest to the "SHIVERS" logo and
design are owned by River Publishing, Inc. No
portion of the "SHIVERS" logo and design may be
reproduced in part or whole without prior written
permission from River Publishing, Inc. An
application for a registered trademark of the
"SHIVERS" logo and design is pending with the
Federal Patent and Trademark office.

30926

Chapter One

Kerri nervously closed the door to the tiny bookstore. As she did, the hinges creaked and a little bell hanging above the door tinkled pleasantly.

But this was not a pleasant shop. Kerri looked around, peering through the shadows and the dust.

What kind of place was this, anyway?

It didn't look like any bookstore she had ever been inside before. Deep shadows carved hollows from the bare walls and wooden floor. Cobwebs dangled from the ceiling. Three short bookcases — just *three* in the whole shop! — contained old dusty volumes with broken spines, books that looked as if they hadn't been read in decades.

It seemed far too dark in this store for reading, anyway.

Kerri glanced again at the sign painted on the glass of the door. Yes, this was the right place: Harriman's Book Shoppe.

Her older sister, Erin, had asked for something from Harriman's as a gift for her thirteenth birthday. Anything at all, so long as it came from that one shop. No other bookstore, Erin had insisted, would carry the kind of book she really wanted.

So Kerri had taken money she earned doing chores for neighbors and ventured into the city by herself, a bold eleven-year-old hopping a crowded metro bus and riding all the way downtown, following a map to 1275 Adding Place — the address of Harriman's Book Shoppe.

It sat on a quiet, dead-end alley.

But where *was* everyone? There were no customers, no clerks. Not even an owner anywhere in sight. It was as if no one at all worked in the dark, dirty store.

"Hello?" Kerri called out. "Hello? Is anyone here?"

No response. No sound. Nothing.

Kerri walked uncertainly across the floor toward the bookcases in the rear of the store. The boards beneath her feet groaned loudly and — for an instant — she thought something moved behind her. From the corner of one eye, she thought she had seen a black form turn just a bit, shift position slightly.

Someone was here after all! Someone who was trying to hide from her!

She snapped her head around to confront the mysterious person — but saw nothing. Only the filthy, shadowed shop contrasted with the bright sunshine that spread over the alley outside the windows.

"Hello?" Kerri called again. "Does anyone work here? Hellllloooo!"

Still, there was no answer.

With an expression of disgust, Kerri carefully slid one of the books from the grimy shelves, brushing a thick layer of dust off the cover with a swipe of her palm.

𝕿𝖍𝖊 𝕿𝖊𝖗𝖗𝖎𝖇𝖑𝖊 𝕿𝖊𝖗𝖗𝖔𝖗 𝕭𝖔𝖔𝖐, the

front jacket said beneath the dust.

What an odd title, Kerri thought. It didn't seem to make any sense. Wasn't terror *always* terrible?

Or was this a book about some terror even more terrible than most?

She shrugged her shoulders and started to put the book back onto the shelf.

Then, out of nowhere, three bony fingers wrapped tightly around her hand and began to squeeze.

Kerri screamed and spun wildly to face her attacker.

She only found an old woman, smiling kindly. The woman was very thin and very short, perhaps only four and a half feet high. She was hunched over badly from age, so that she appeared even shorter than her true height. She had thin gray hair and wore a red and black bandanna over her head.

She stood looking at Kerri, still holding her hand.

"Hello, my child," she said in a soft, hoarse voice. "I can see you are a fine judge of literature."

Kerri was so shocked by the old woman's sudden appearance and unusual looks that for a few moments she could only stammer.

"I — uh, that is, I — Excuse me, um, what I mean is — " she began, pulling her hand free. "I — I, um, I'm sorry for screaming like that, ma'am. I called out for someone when I came into the store but no one answered."

"Forgive me, child," the old woman said. "I'm very hard of hearing these days. And as you can see, I'm also rather short of stature. I was standing behind one of the bookshelves, looking at an old volume when you came in. You must not have seen me there. And I'm afraid I didn't hear the bell on the door — or even hear you call for assistance. Forgive me, please. I don't mean to be unhelpful."

"That's all right, ma'am," Kerri said. "It's just so dark in here and — well, when I didn't see anyone, I became a little frightened. I'm sorry."

"Perfectly understandable, my child. Perfectly understandable," the old woman croaked softly. A thin, sweet smile creased her lips. "I take it that you've come to my shop to purchase a book. A birthday gift perhaps?"

"Well, yes, that's — A birthday gift? Is that what you said?" Kerri asked. "That's amazing. How did you know that?"

"Oh, I think you must have mentioned it to me, my child," the old woman said. "A birthday gift for your older sister, I think you said."

"No, I didn't say that. I didn't tell you anything," Kerri said. "How could you know that?"

"As one gets older, my child, one comes to know many things," the old woman answered mysteriously. "Too many things, perhaps. Too many things."

"But I just don't understand how . . . " Kerri began.

"Come, let's look at that book in your hand," the old woman interrupted. "You've made a fine choice there, my child. You are an excellent judge of good books."

"Well, I haven't really chosen anything yet,"

Kerri replied. "This is just the first book I happened to pick up. I'd like to look at some others before I buy anything."

"You must always trust your instincts, child. Learn to listen to the inner voice that moves you. There is always a reason," the old woman said. "You have chosen the finest book in my shop — the perfect selection for your sister, my dear. It will give her everything she wanted from a book. And more. Much more."

"But I just don't get it, ma'am," Kerri said. "I don't mean to be rude. It's just that you talk as if you know exactly what kind of book my sister wanted. But you don't even *know* my sister. How can you have any idea what type of gift she would enjoy?"

"I *do* know what kind of book your sister wants, my child," the old woman replied. "It is what *all* the boys and girls who come into my shop want to purchase. They all come for the same reason. They want a book that is more than just an ordinary book. A book that is special."

"Yes, that's right," Kerri said. "My sister said

you carry special books."

"That is true, my dear. Harriman's carries only special books," the old woman said hoarsely. "We stock only tales of horror and death, frightening stories to make you shiver with fear as you read them. Just what every child wants today, I understand. But the books on *these* shelves are different from any you can buy at other stores. My books make readers feel things no other literature ever could make them feel. My books make readers think things no other literature ever has made them think. Yes, my child, these books are special. And you have chosen the perfect volume for Erin."

"Erin?" Kerri said, surprised. "How did you know her . . . "

"Come over here, child, and you can pay me for the book and be on your way," the old woman interrupted, walking slowly toward the dusty cash register. "Your sister is a lucky girl to have this for a birthday gift. You are very kind to buy it for her."

"But I — I haven't even looked inside the book yet," Kerri protested. She felt strangely frightened. She thought of putting the book down and running wildly out of the store.

But why? The old woman had done nothing to her, she thought. There was no reason to be foolish. So she remained.

"It's just that I — well, I don't know how much the book costs anyway," she said. "I might not be able to afford it."

"You have made a wise choice. Your sister will find the book most exciting," the old woman responded, stepping behind the counter to accept Kerri's money. "That volume costs exactly eight dollars, my child. Not a penny more."

"Eight dollars, you said? That's really odd," Kerri replied. "I have exactly eight dollars in my pocket. That's all the money I earned doing chores."

"Ahhhh, good then," the old woman said, holding out her hand. "You can afford my little book after all. Eight dollars, please."

"I think I should at least look through the book before I buy it," Kerri said. "My father's a businessman.

He always says you should never buy anything without looking it over carefully."

The old woman's bony fingers quickly wrapped around Kerri's hand again, pulling it away from the book.

"Trust me, my child," she said, with a kindly smile. "You have selected the finest work in Harriman's Book Shoppe. But don't you think your sister must be the first to read it? It is, after all, her birthday gift. Please, dear. You must do as I say: Take the book straight home and give it to your sister. Do not read even one word of it first by yourself. Do not allow anyone other than your sister to read it first. Give the book to Erin. She must be the first person to open the volume. Please remember that!"

"Well, y-yes, of course. I'll, uh, do that," Kerri said, flustered. She reached for her money. All she really wanted was to leave Harriman's as quickly as possible with a birthday gift for her sister — and to never return to the dirty, weird old shop.

"You have selected wisely among all my volumes," the old woman croaked, still smiling. "You have picked the very best book for your sister. It will be a birthday present your sweet sister will never, ever forget! Give it to darling Erin tonight. From that moment on, she will keep it always with her — right until the end of her life!"

Chapter Two

As Kerri walked through the back door of her home into the kitchen, her mother was just putting thirteen candles into Erin's birthday cake — a thick chocolate cake with chocolate icing. Erin's favorite kind! And Kerri's too!

"Where have you *been*?" her mother asked irritably. "We've been worried about you, Kerri! You know you're supposed to be home for supper by five o'clock. Just because your father's out of town on business doesn't mean you can do anything you like."

"I'm sorry, Mom," Kerri said. "It wasn't because Dad's not home. The buses from downtown were running late because of a big traffic jam. I went down to a bookstore to get Erin's gift. I got just what she wanted — a book from this really weird shop in a little alley. See, here it is. I don't know why Erin wanted something from this place, though. She must be jerkier than I thought. It was so creepy at that store, Mom! Everything's dusty and dirty. I hated it!"

"Well, you almost missed celebrating your sister's birthday," her mother said, lighting the candles. "I'm very angry with you for going downtown alone and then being late. We'll talk about this later. Come on. Bring your gift and hold the door for me while I carry the cake into the dining room."

As they walked into the dining room together, Kerri and her mother began to sing:

"Haaaappy Birthday to you! Haaaappy Birthday to you! Haaaappy birthday, dear Errriiiin! Haaaappy birthday to yoooouuuu!"

It was a small celebration — Erin, Kerri, their mother, plus the family dog, Buster. Two of Erin's closest friends were also there. Laurie and Kimberly were in the same grade as Erin, and each lived just a few houses away.

The three friends were almost inseparable, eating lunches together at school, doing homework together in the evening, playing together every day during summer vacations.

Of course, all three felt that Kerri was much too young and immature to spend time with them. They went out of their way to exclude her from their activities.

This hurt Kerri's feelings — and she disliked and resented Laurie and Kimberly because of it.

So Kerri was not pleased to find them sitting in her dining room, singing "Happy Birthday" along with the family. Her smile collapsed, replaced by a bitter scowl.

And when Erin saw Kerri scowling at her best friends, the birthday girl's grin dissolved into an expression of annoyance.

This was how things often went between the two siblings. As much as they loved each other — and they loved each other very much — Erin and Kerri couldn't seem to get along.

They bickered over who would use the bathroom first in the mornings. They argued over whose turn it was to wash the dishes. They fought over who had last taken Buster for a walk.

Erin was forever calling her younger sister a "baby." Kerri was forever calling her older sister a "jerk."

Neither was true: Kerri wasn't a baby and Erin wasn't a jerk. Both were just regular kids trying to fit in with friends and classmates, competing for the attention of their parents, and hoping to act at least a year or two older than they really were.

Inevitably, these struggles led to frustrations with each other — and the frustrations bubbled over into fights.

"*Moooomm*! What are *they* doing here?" Kerri asked. "You said this was going to be just for the family tonight."

"Kerri, will you just grow up for once and stop acting like a baby!" Erin said. "Be polite! Kimberly and Laurie are here because I asked them to join us."

"Hi, Kerri," Laurie and Kimberly said together

— in a syrupy voice intended to irritate Kerri.

"Hi," Kerri said dully.

"Kerri, you're in enough trouble as it is," her mother warned. "Now shape up and mind your manners or you can just go spend the rest of the evening in your room doing homework."

"Yes, Mom," Kerri said.

"Besides, it's *my* birthday," Erin pointed out. "Maybe you could think about *me* for once and try to be nice to me for a change."

"I was trying to be nice to you, you jerk," Kerri said. "That's why I'm in trouble and missed dinner and everything."

She held out the small paper bag which held the book.

"See this?" she asked. "I tried to get something you really wanted. And all you can say is how I'm not being nice to you on your birthday. Here, take it."

"Presents come a little later, honey," their mother said. "After we all have some cake. OK, Erin. Make a wish and blow the candles out!"

After everyone ate a large slice of chocolate cake, their mother handed Erin two gift-wrapped boxes.

Erin ripped them open, discovering a red party dress in one and two short-sleeved silk tops in the other. They were just the clothes she had wanted. She kissed her mother gratefully as Buster wagged his tail and happily shredded wrapping paper on the floor.

The packages from the two guests were next. Laurie gave her friend a gift certificate good for three free movies at the local theater and Kimberly handed over a large flowering plant for Erin's room, a tall amaryllis.

Erin thanked them each, smiling as she admired her presents.

Finally, Kerri passed the paper bag over the table to her sister.

"Here," she said, as if she didn't care whether Erin liked the present or not. "This is my gift. I bought it with my own money. Sorry I didn't get a chance to wrap it."

Erin slipped the book out of the bag, and stared

at the title: 𝕿𝖍𝖊 𝕿𝖊𝖗𝖗𝖎𝖇𝖑𝖊 𝕿𝖊𝖗𝖗𝖔𝖗 𝕭𝖔𝖔𝖐.

She sat there looking at the cover without a word or a smile.

"It's still kinda dusty," Kerri said. "I tried to clean it off on the bus ride home. I know it's old. But you wanted something from that store, Harriman's — and everything in there was really old. The woman at the store said it was the best book she had. I hope you like it."

"Are you *kidding*?" Erin said. "I *love* it! Wow! I can't believe you went all the way to Harriman's and bought this with your own money. Thanks, Kerri! This is so cool!"

Erin gave her sister an enthusiastic hug and kiss. Kerri hugged her back.

"What's so cool about an old used book?" Kimberly said. "I don't get it."

"Me either," Laurie said. "What is this place, Harriman's? I've never heard of it."

"I haven't been there," Erin said. "But I heard there's no other book shop like it. I met someone who told me that it's the only store with very special scary books — things you can't even find in a library."

"Really?" Kimberly said.

"Wow," Laurie said.

"Yeah, I met this person about a month ago when I was in another store buying a Shivers book," Erin said. "I was getting *The Spider Kingdom*, I think. Anyway, this lady made me feel like I just *had* to have a book from Harriman's. She told me that if I wanted the scariest books in the world, even scarier than Shivers, Harriman's was the only place to go."

"Wow, scarier than Shivers?" Laurie responded. "Those are really spooky stories. Oooooh! I want a book from Harriman's, too!"

"Yeah, that's why I've wanted to go there ever since," Erin said. "But I didn't have a chance to get downtown. So I was telling Kerri about it when she asked what I wanted for my birthday. I can't believe she actually went all the way down there!"

"You said some lady told you about Harriman's?" Kerri asked. Suddenly, she felt uncomfortable again.

"Yeah, that's right," Erin said. "Just some lady in another store. Why?"

"It probably doesn't matter," Kerri said. "But what kind of lady was she? What did she look like?"

"I dunno. She was just real old. Kind of all hunched over, I guess," Erin said, still looking at the book cover. "I only saw her for a minute or two. Besides, who cares?"

"I just need to know, that's all," Kerri replied. "What else do you remember about her? Think, Erin! What did she look like?"

"Well, I remember she was really short for a grown lady and her shoulders were all hunched over," Erin said. "And she had gray hair covered by a black and red bandanna. And I remember thinking that she had really bony fingers."

"That's her!" Kerri exclaimed. "That's the same woman who waited on me at Harriman's! She was really weird and it was so scary because we were in this dark, strange bookstore. And she kept saying weird things like she knew who I was and who I was buying this book for!"

"You know, now that you mention it, she seemed kinda strange to me, too," Erin said, rubbing her lip nervously. "It was like she wasn't there one second, and the next second she was standing right next to me. She sort of showed up out of nowhere and started talking about scary books."

"Showed up out of nowhere?" their mother laughed. "That's silly."

"No really, Mom," Erin said. "That's how it seemed. There was no one behind me, then all of a sudden, there she was. She put her bony fingers on my hand. And she used my name — I remember she called me 'Erin' and I could never understand how she knew me."

"It's true, Mom!" Kerri said. "This old lady knew who I was buying the book for and how old Erin was and everything!"

"It really was weird," Erin agreed. "I just remember that she took my hand as I reached for a Shivers book and she said something like, 'You must go to Harriman's Book Shoppe, my child. If you want stories of true terror, Harriman's is the finest store in the world.' "

"That's her!" Kerri said. "That's just how she talked to me, Mom!"

"Yeah, and she said something else, too," Erin recalled. "She said, 'You won't be disappointed by a book from Harriman's, my dear. You will find true terror in it. A terror that will seem more real to you than your most frightening nightmares!' "

Chapter Three

It was nearly midnight.

The birthday celebration had ended just two hours earlier. After helping to clean up the mess, Erin was alone in her room at last, one small lamp spilling a dim light into the blackness that surrounded her.

She sat on her bed, staring at the cover of the slender volume from Harriman's Book Shoppe: **The Terrible Terror Book.**

Somehow she felt afraid to open it now, afraid to begin reading the horrifying story that would unfold, afraid even to glance at the first words of the first page.

She couldn't forget how the same old woman who had told her about Harriman's — and had mysteriously called her by name! — also worked at the shop and knew exactly why Kerri was buying the book and who it was for.

How could that happen? Who was this old woman? What kind of book was this?

These questions appeared deep and shadowy; as shadowy as the strange book shop Kerri had described to her — and the only possible answers seemed absurd.

Erin still stared fearfully at the book cover, still refusing to open it.

Until finally, filled with dread, she stretched out her thumb and index finger and carefully pulled back the cover.

Inside, on the very first page, she saw these words:

"Whoever first opens this cover and begins to read

"Must continue this tale to the bitter end —

"And for safety, best finish it with utmost speed.

"No matter how terrible the story you'll hear

"Read each word, each sentence, to the very last —

"Or die a horrible death, alone with your fear!"

Erin gasped — and dropped the book as if it were made of hot lead.

"Oh, how terrible!" she gasped. "What have I done? I have some kind of awful book here — and now I have to read it or I'll die!"

She fought off the panic that surged through her, trying to breathe slowly to calm herself down. Maybe she was being foolish, she thought.

After all, this *was* a scary book. It was *supposed* to be frightening.

And the old lady had promised that it would be more frightening than anything else she'd ever read.

Of course, that was all there was to it! This was just part of the fun — just a really scary introduction to a really scary story. Big deal!

Erin found her confidence returning. She laughed at herself. How ridiculous she had been!

"I can't believe I actually fell for that goofy warning at the beginning. Sheesh!" she mumbled to herself. "But I have to admit, it got me for a second. This is probably going to be a great book!"

She opened the book again and began to flip toward the first chapter when she heard a soft tapping at her door.

Who could that be at so late an hour?

"Pssst! Erin. It's me," Kerri called. "Let me in!"

"What do you want? It's late," Erin said, unlocking her door and letting in her sister and the family dog, Buster. "You should be asleep."

"Yeah, but I couldn't sleep," Kerri said. "I was worried. I was lying in bed with Buster, thinking about that book I gave you. And, uh — well, the thing is — well, I just don't think you should read it!"

"Why not?" Erin asked. "It looks like fun."

"Because of something that weird old lady told me," Kerri said. "She said to bring the book right home and give it to you — and not to read any of it myself. She said I shouldn't read even one word of it before you. I think there's something really strange about this book, Erin. I don't want you to even open it."

"Too late for that," Erin said. "I already did. And yeah, it starts off kind of creepy. It has some weird warning saying that whoever first opens the cover must finish the book or die. But then I understood that was just part of the scary story. Nothing to be afraid of."

"I'm not so sure, Erin," Kerri said. "This whole thing with the old lady and the stuff she knew about us — it gives me the creeps big-time!"

"Look, Kerri, it's just a book," Erin said, picking up the dusty volume. "Just a leather cover, some paper pages and ink. How could a book possibly hurt me? How could something so totally innocent actually cause me any . . . "

Erin didn't get a chance to finish her words.

Because at that very moment, her entire body began to shake with a fierce convulsion!

It was as if the book had somehow become electrified — and was sending 20,000 volts through her body!

"H-h-help!" she shouted, her voice weak and

ragged from the power coursing out of the terrible book and through her flesh. "Heeeeelllpp m-m-meeee, K-k-k-kerrri! I'm d-d-dying! The b-b-book is k-killing me! H-h-heeellpp!"

Chapter Four

Kerri had no idea what to do.

She tried to scream for help from her mother, but she was so horrified by what was happening to Erin that she couldn't make a sound.

Buster began to bark, upset and confused by the sight of Erin's convulsion.

Kerri knew that if you touched someone who was receiving an electrical shock, you would receive a shock too. Unless, of course, you were shielded from the current by touching the victim with a piece of rubber.

But there seemed to be nothing made of rubber anywhere in sight.

"Oh, no!" she squeaked helplessly. "What can I do?"

Frantic, she grabbed a pencil from her sister's desk and tried to poke the book out of Erin's hand with the rubber eraser.

Once! Twice! Three, four, five times! She lunged at the book cover as if attempting to spear it on a sharp sword, but Erin held on tightly, fused to the powerful electric shock of the terrible, terrible book.

Suddenly Erin burst out laughing!

"Ha, ha, ha, ha, ha!" she cackled. "Did I get you or what? I really had you going!"

Instantly, Kerri realized that her sister had tricked her. She felt furious.

"Ha, ha," she said angrily. "Very funny, scaring me to death. You really are a jerk. Buster! Stop barking!"

"I'm sorry, Kerri!" Erin laughed. "I just couldn't resist. I didn't mean to freak you out or anything. It was just a joke."

"Yeah, some joke — as if you'd like it if someone did that to you!" Kerri shot back. "And you call *me* a baby! I think *you're* the one who's immature."

"OK, I said I was sorry," Erin replied. "It was just a joke."

"Well, I'm going to bed," Kerri said in a huff. "Go ahead and read that terror book if you want to. See if I care! You big jerk."

With that, Kerri called Buster and slammed her sister's bedroom door — or at least, slammed it as loudly as she could without waking up their mother.

"Baby!" Erin called out.

Alone again, she sat on her bed, opened *The Terrible Terror Book* and started to read Chapter One:

"The night was warm.

"Yes, very warm indeed. And all the windows of the large home were open wide to let in whatever slight breezes stirred the hot summer air," the book began.

Erin paused to wipe her brow and sip from a cup of water, then realized that it really was a warm summer night outside — and that all the windows of her large home were open wide, just as in the book. And she noticed that hardly any breezes stirred the humid summer air.

Hmmmm, she thought. That's odd.

She looked down and started to read again:

"The two sisters had just had another fight — though it was not their first disagreement of the day. Kerrin and her younger sister, Terri, often argued over the smallest things, though they loved each other very much.

"Still, they could not seem to get along. Now, Terri was sulking in her room, late at night with the family dog, Mustard, as Kerrin sat alone in her own bedroom, reading the latest horror book she had purchased.

"It was a black, moonless night outside — and as she read, Kerrin began to feel uneasy.

"Something bad was about to happen. She just knew it."

Erin paused, swallowing nervously as she glanced around the room. This *was* a scary book! But she was eager to continue reading:

"Suddenly, a stiff wind clattered through the trees outside her window — accompanied by a loud

snap.

    "And a scream!

    "It was her sister, Terri. Something bad had happened all right.

    "The strong wind had blown shut Terri's bedroom window, just as the young girl had rested her hand on the windowsill to feel the thick summer air. She was bleeding and crying when Kerrin ran to her. Mustard was barking uneasily at the commotion."

    What a strange story, Erin thought. Kerrin and Terri? Sisters who fought all the time? Well, at least there were no real winds outside to worry about, Erin thought.

    The night air was completely still.

    All at once, a stiff wind rattled the branches outside her window, banging the storm shutters and shaking the cedar shingles.

    Suddenly, she heard a loud crash!

    And a scream!

    It was Kerri!

    Erin flew out of her bed, flinging open her door

and running to her sister's room. Kerri stood there crying, holding out her right hand. It was bleeding.

"Owww!" she cried. "Ow! Ow! I hurt my hand."

Buster barked nervously.

Erin stood stock still, frozen with fear.

"Oh, no," she said quietly. "This can't be happening!"

Chapter Five

"Erin!" Kerri whined. "Help me! Why are you just standing there?"

"Huh? Oh, I'm sorry, Kerri," Erin said, coming out of her terrified trance. "I'll run to the bathroom and get some bandages. Wait here!"

Fortunately, the incident had not awakened their mother, who slept at the opposite end of the long upstairs hallway. The girls wouldn't have to explain why they were still awake so late.

Erin put some alcohol on her sister's cut and wrapped the hand tightly in a bandage as Kerri explained how she had gotten hurt.

"It was stupid, I guess," she said. "I stuck my hand out the window to feel if there was any breeze. It was so hot and I couldn't sleep after our fight. I was just resting my hand on the windowsill when a gust of wind must have loosened my window. 'Cause it came crashing down on my hand!"

"Why were you resting your hand there?" Erin demanded angrily. "That was really stupid!"

"Don't get *mad* at me, Erin!" Kerri said. "I didn't mean for it to happen. Why are you yelling at me?"

"Oh, never mind!" Erin replied, walking toward the bathroom to put away the bandages and alcohol. "You wouldn't believe me anyway. I must be losing my mind! Just go to sleep, Kerri!"

But Erin knew she wasn't losing her mind. She felt sure there was something very, very strange about her new horror book — something she didn't even want to think about.

It was all just a weird coincidence, right? The similar names and similar weather and similar accident? It *had* to be a coincidence!

This was an old book — a *very* old book, judging by its appearance. It must have been written at least fifty years ago, Erin thought. How could it have any connection with things that were happening *now*?

Uneasily, she lay down on her bed. Almost as if she couldn't help herself, she opened *The Terrible Terror Book* once more. And she started to read:

"But this was only the beginning of the terrible things that were about to happen to Kerrin and Terri and their family. Only the beginning of the long nightmare that would blacken the days ahead.

"There was to be more pain, more sorrow. And more blood, Kerrin felt certain.

"Much, much more blood."

Erin looked away from her book, too frightened to continue reading.

It just *couldn't* be true, she thought. This was only a silly book, after all. It had nothing to do with her!

It couldn't have anything to do with her, right? It just *couldn't*!

It couldn't *possibly* have anything to do with *her*!

Then, against her will, three frightening words popped into Erin's mind: Or *could* it?

Chapter Six

Erin had fallen asleep without undressing for the night, drifting off worriedly with the new book laying open over her stomach.

She had not been able to read another wo[rd] the horror story. But she also couldn't bring her[self] close the book and never open it again — not aft[er] *Terrible Terror Book's* terrifying introduction.

Those fifty-three words were seared into her memory:

"Whoever first opens this cover and begins to read

"Must continue this tale to the bitter end —
"And for safety, best finish it with utmost speed.
"No matter how terrible the story you'll hear
"Read each word, each sentence, to the very

last —

"Or die a horrible death, alone with your fear!"

It was impossible to ignore a warning that sounded so ominous. "A horrible death," it said. "Alone with your fear!"

She *had* to keep reading, no matter what — even though she wanted to rip out each page and burn it to ashes in the family fireplace.

Fearfully, she sat up in her bed and looked with dread at the book cover stretched out in her hands.

Outside, the warm summer sun bathed the trees and grass in fresh light. Birds chirped merry little songs. It was a beautiful day — everywhere, that is, except inside Erin's tormented heart.

Picking up *The Terrible Terror Book* slowly, she began to read from its worn pages once more:

"Kerrin was frightened.

"Why were the bad things happening to her? What had her family done to deserve this curse?

"And what was going to happen next? If only

she knew, maybe she could somehow prevent it!

"*But all that Kerrin knew for sure was that the curse was just starting to work its terror. Somehow she felt this with absolute certainty.*

"*Then a horrible thought came to her: her mother! She was the next victim!*

"*Yes, her mother was climbing on a ladder outside their home, washing windows in the summer sunshine, accompanied by Mustard, the family dog. It was a beautiful day, Mother had said, to get some cleaning accomplished around their house.*

"*Kerrin shoved her feet quickly into a pair of sneakers and ran downstairs in a flash. She had to find her mother and warn her — she had to make her mother come off that ladder!*

" '*Mom! Mom! Get down, right now!*' *she called, running toward the ladder. Her mother was reaching toward a second-story bathroom window, sponge in hand.*

" '*What? What are you yelling about?*' *her mother asked. '*I'm busy, Kerrin!*'*

"Mustard began to bark.

" 'I know, Mom. But you have to get down from there! I can't explain why — but I just know something's going to happen if you don't,' Kerrin begged breathlessly.

" 'Now don't be absurd, Kerrin!' her mother answered. 'I'm fine! I just want to reach across here and wash this . . . '

"But as Kerrin's mother looked down toward her daughter, she lost her balance. She dropped the sponge and grabbed desperately for the ladder — but too late!

"She flipped backward and spun toward the ground like an Olympic diver off a springboard, landing with a fierce slam on her back and shoulder. The ladder fell on top of her, spilling the bucket of water that had dangled from a clip.

"Kerrin screamed — then yelled for Terri to call an ambulance. Their mother's shoulder and back were badly hurt. The nightmare of mishaps and misfortunes was getting worse."

Just then, Erin heard a metallic rattle outside. She put the book down on her lap.

There it was again, the sound of metal clanking on their lawn.

Suddenly Erin understood — and leaped from bed to peer out her window.

What she saw sent an icy surge of fear through her veins: Her mother was cleaning the windows of their home, standing near the top of a tall ladder!

With a thick sponge in one hand, she was reaching out to wash the windows of a second-story bathroom!

"Mom! Get down!" Erin hollered frantically. "Get down right now!"

Buster began to bark.

"Hi, honey!" her mother called back with a smile. "Sorry, I can't hear you! It's such a nice day, I wanted to get some cleaning done around the house!"

"Mom, get down! Get down!" Erin shouted, gesturing toward the ground.

Her mother only smiled again and waved — but

she waved so enthusiastically she lost her balance!

The ladder tilted away from the side of the house and began to sway back and forth. Her mother dropped the sponge and screamed in panic!

Then she spun backwards off the ladder, toppling wildly to the grass below. She landed on her back and shoulder with a hard thud.

Erin screamed!

"Kerri! Kerri! Dial 911! Get an ambulance! Mom's hurt!" she cried, wiggling her feet into a pair of sneakers.

She ran downstairs to help her mother, who looked desperately injured.

It was really happening. It was true after all!

The nightmare was getting *worse* — and it wasn't just in some story.

The Terrible Terror Book was making terrible things happen for real — to her!

Chapter Seven

"Close the door, Kerri!" Erin whispered. "I don't want Mom to hear us."

Kerri did as her sister asked, then sat down on Erin's bed. Laurie and Kimberly were already there. All three girls were nervous, wondering why Erin had called them together for an "emergency meeting."

Erin paced around her room for a moment, rubbing her lip worriedly, then leaned close to the girls.

"OK, listen carefully, all right?" she whispered, glancing toward her door. "This is going to sound crazy. But you've got to try to believe me. OK?"

"Yeah, sure," Laurie said.

"Of course, Erin," Kimberly answered.

Kerri just nodded.

"Ever since Mom fell off that ladder and broke

her shoulder yesterday, I've been thinking about something," Erin said. "Something very, very weird. It's something that's happening because of this book."

She held up *The Terrible Terror Book*. All three girls shrank back from her as though she had just shown them a big, hairy tarantula.

"I knew it!" Kerri said. "I knew there was something weird about that book."

"You were right, sis," Erin said. "This is a really scary book, just like that old lady said it would be. But it's not scary because of the story. It's scary because whatever I read in this book comes true!"

"What?" Kimberly and Laurie exclaimed.

"That's nuts," Kerri said.

"I told you it was going to sound crazy," Erin said. "But I'm telling you guys the truth. If you don't believe me, just listen to this!"

She read them portions of the tale about the fictional girls Kerrin and Terri — the passage where the window dropped onto Terri's hand, and the section where the mother fell from the ladder.

The girls grabbed *The Terrible Terror Book* from Erin's hands and read those parts for themselves, making absolutely sure the words they had just heard Erin read were really printed in black and white.

And, of course, they were. When they saw this, Kerri and Kimberly and Laurie were instantly convinced. They knew Erin was telling the truth about the horrible book.

"You have to destroy that book — right away!" Kimberly said.

"Throw it in your fireplace and burn it!" Laurie said.

"Why haven't you torn it up already, Erin?" Kerri asked frantically. "Just throw it in the garbage or something and get it out of our house! I don't want to look at it!"

"Don't you think I already thought of that?" Erin said. "I wish I could destroy it. But I can't! Listen to this."

She read them the frightening warning on the first page.

"Wow!" Laurie and Kimberly slowly said together. Their eyes grew wide. Now they understood Erin's terrible dilemma.

"This is too weird, sis!" Kerri said, her voice quavering, tears forming in her eyes. "What are we gonna do?"

"I don't know, Kerri," Erin said. "All I know is that I have to keep reading the book, or I'll die!" Erin said, a tear of her own streaking down her cheek. "But I also know that, if I keep reading it, more bad things will happen to people I love — and probably to me, too!"

"No matter what you do, you lose," Laurie breathed.

"This is terrible!" Kimberly said angrily.

"We can't tell Mom about this," Kerri said. "She'd freak out! Especially with Dad away on business. And her arm in a sling and all. She's all alone with us here."

"I know," Erin agreed. "We have to find some way to deal with this book ourselves. But *how*?"

No one answered. They sat in silence as the

question hung in the air. All of them worked their minds now, looking for solutions. Long minutes passed without any of them speaking a single word.

"I don't see any way at all," Kimberly said finally. "If bad things happen when you read it — and you have to read it or die — what can you do? You've just *got* to read it."

"I've got an idea!" Kerri said. "The only person who possibly could help us is the old lady at the book shop. She's the one who knows about the power of this book. She can do something to break this curse. Maybe she could give me my money and take the book back. That way, you won't *have* to read it!"

"That's a good idea, Kerri!" Laurie said. "Or maybe the old lady can at least exchange this book for something less scary. I'm sure she could do *something* to help if we asked her to!"

"But remember? I have to keep reading *this* book or die!" Erin wailed. "And who knows what bad things it will make happen to us next? I'm scared to leave the house."

"We have to go to Harriman's," Kerri said. "Besides, the book doesn't say how fast you have to read it. The introduction only says it's safest to read quickly. You've gone since yesterday without reading any more of it and nothing has happened. I don't think you should read another word until we get downtown on the bus — and take this book back to Harriman's!"

"I agree," Kimberly said. "It's the only choice we have. Come on, there's no use wasting time. Laurie and I will go with you. We're friends. We should stick together through stuff like this."

The four girls headed out the door, saying goodbye to Erin and Kerri's mother as if they were only going outside to enjoy the sunny day. Instead, they walked quickly to the bus stop and hopped on the large blue-and-white Number Thirteen bus that would carry them downtown.

Erin held *The Terrible Terror Book* anxiously on her lap for the entire one-hour ride. It frightened her even to look at it, much less hold it. The cover actually felt hot against her legs, as if an invisible fire burned inside the pages. It really was a terrible book, she thought. A terrible, terrible terror book!

At last, the Number Thirteen bus arrived among the skyscrapers of downtown. The four girls clambered down the steps and rushed toward the alley known as Adding Place.

Kerri held the map she originally had used to find the bookstore. She referred to it often as the girls passed street after street after street. It was a longer walk than she remembered.

"Here it is," she said finally, looking at a street sign. "Adding Place. We turn down here. The store's right at the end of this little alley."

But as they neared the end of the alley, Kerri realized something was wrong.

"Oh, no!" she shouted. "It can't be! I was just here a couple days ago! No, no, *no!*"

"What's wrong, Kerri?" Erin asked worriedly.

"Look! That's what's wrong," Kerri said, pointing over at the small glass door with the numbers 1-2-7-5 overhead. "That's it! That's Harriman's Book

Shoppe!"

Shocked, the four girls slowly walked to the glass door and peered in hopelessly. They couldn't believe their eyes.

There was absolutely nothing inside 1275 Adding Place!

No book shelves, no front counter, no cash register. Not even the words "Harriman's Book Shoppe" painted on the glass door.

Only cobwebs and dust and filth. The ceiling tiles were falling down. The wooden floor had a huge hole in it, as though the boards had rotted away and collapsed from long neglect.

"Are you *sure* this is the place?" Kimberly asked in a trembling voice.

"Positive!" Kerri replied, her eyes wide with horror. "This is where I bought Erin's book just two days ago! It's impossible! But it's true!"

"B-b-but, Kerri, it just *can't* be the place," Erin stammered miserably. "Look at this dump! Anyone can see that this store has been abandoned. No human being has set foot inside here for at least ten years!"

Chapter Eight

"This is too weird for me," Laurie said. "I think we should get out of here!"

"Me, too!" said Kimberly.

"Come on, you guys," said Erin with a weak laugh. "There has to be some explanation for this Kerri, this must be the wrong street. You're scaring us to death and it has to be your mistake. How could there have been a bookstore here two days ago? You're wrong."

"No, I'm *not* wrong!" Kerri shot back. "Look at the street sign for yourself. Adding Place, it says. And this is 1275 Adding Place. Isn't that the same address you gave me? And I remember this door. This was the bookstore, Erin! Don't call me a liar, you big jerk!"

"Shut up, you stupid baby!" Erin said.

"Hey, this is no time for you guys to start an argument," Laurie said. "Let's just get out of here before something else weird happens!"

"Maybe you're right," Erin agreed. "Come on. Let's go!"

The girls turned and began to walk slowly away from the door. After a step or two, they walked faster, then faster. Then they began to run.

In their rush, *The Terrible Terror Book* slipped from Erin's hand and skidded across the alley.

At that moment, the girls heard an odd noise — a loud creaking and the tinkling of a tiny bell somewhere along the street.

They turned. The door to 1275 Adding Place was open!

It was open wide, as if it had been pushed by a strong wind or a stealthy hand. But not a wisp of wind stirred anywhere.

"H-how did that get open?" Laurie asked. "D-didn't you try to open it, K-Kerri?"

"Y-yeah, I *tried* to open the door," Kerri said. "But it was locked."

"That's what I thought," Erin said.

"Yeah. M-me, too," Kimberly said.

They gazed at each other blankly, bewildered and afraid. Yet somehow they felt drawn toward that beckoning door. It held for them the horrible yet irresistible fascination of staring into an open grave.

One by one, they started to drift toward the doorway — first Erin, then Kerri, then Kimberly, then Laurie. Without a word, they floated like four puffs of smoke down the alley, closer and closer to 1275 Adding Place.

The puffs collected into one cloud at the threshold of the abandoned book shop. The girls bunched together into a single mass of trembling arms and shaking legs, of twitching mouths and darting eyes.

"D-do you, uh, th-think we ought to just go in?" Laurie asked. "I mean, w-we'll be trespassing, you know."

"Th-that's t-true," Kimberly agreed.

"Well, I'm going in," Kerri said boldly.

The other girls followed her inside the bookstore, their eyes glancing up and down as they stepped gingerly into the gloomy, dust-filled room.

"This is very strange," Kerri said slowly. Her words seemed to echo in the emptiness of the abandoned store. "I remember the old lady standing right there when I paid for the book."

"It smells bad in here," Kimberly said. "Like a musty attic no one has cleaned in years."

"It didn't smell like that two days ago," Kerri said. "And it sure didn't look like this, either."

"V-very, v-very weird," Erin said. Her teeth clattered as she spoke.

"D-d-definitely," Laurie said, shivering and wrapping her arms around herself.

With no lights, the small shop was even darker than when Kerri had visited before. Instead of deep shadows concealing portions of the store, the store itself was swallowed in one great black shadow. Dust lay three inches thick on the shelves. Cobwebs dangled from the ceiling to the floor.

As their eyes adjusted to the darkness, the girls walked carefully around the enormous hole in the floor and toward the back of the shop.

Suddenly, Kerri noticed a black spiral staircase leading downward.

"Th-that wasn't here before," she said. "I'd remember something like that."

"You're, uh, sure of that, sis?" Erin asked nervously. "No stairs at all?"

"I'm positive," Kerri said. "I walked to the back of the store. There were three bookcases here, filled with old books, but absolutely no staircase!"

"Then this *can't* be the same store you were in!" Laurie protested.

"It *is*!" Kerri insisted.

The girls stared at the spiral stairway for several long moments, their hearts beating fast in their chests, their throats tightening.

"Oh, girls!" a soft, hoarse woman's voice called suddenly. "Come down here, please!"

The girls jumped as if they had been shocked by an electric cattle prod.

"What was that?" Kimberly asked, her voice shaking.

"Helllooo!" Erin called. "Is somebody here?"

"Erin! Kerri! Girls! Come down here, please," the woman's voice answered. "Just down the steps, girls!"

"It's the old lady," Kerri said. "I'd know that voice anywhere. Come on! She's our only hope of getting rid of this awful book!"

Before any of them had a chance to think, they ran to the staircase and tromped down the steps into the darkness below.

A faint light shone from the basement, just enough so the girls could sense the outline of the stairs and find their way to the bottom.

When they reached the cement floor, they all stopped. They stared across the dank, dusty room at the small lamp and wooden rocking chair.

All they could see was a wrinkled hand resting

on the side of the chair, and the back of a head of gray hair wrapped in a red and black bandanna. All else was lost in shadow.

"Come here, my children," the old woman croaked. "A little closer, please."

Shoulder to shoulder, the girls walked nervously toward the old lady. They still could not make out her face.

"Uh, ex-excuse us, ma'am," Kerri began. "I h-hope you don't mind us walking in like this. B-but your door was open."

"That's r-right," Erin continued. "And we w-wanted to, uh, ask about this . . . "

"About this *book*!" the woman's voice interrupted. "Yes, my child. You want me to take it back, is that right, my child? They always do."

"W-well, uh, yes, ma'am," Erin stammered. "If it's not too much trouble."

"No trouble at all, my child," the woman's voice said. "I'll be happy to take back the book, my dear."

With those words, the rocking chair spun

around. The old face flashed into the dim light of the lamp.

But it was not a woman's face at all! It was the face of a shriveled old man!

He was blind, with one of the two eye sockets dark and empty and bloody. His face was smeared with mud and dirt.

He smiled an evil, toothless grin, and laughed.

"I'll take the book — and I'll take you girls too!" he said in the same hoarse female voice. "It'll be so nice to have company to ease my loneliness. Yes, my children, it's so good of you to come to stay with me. Make yourselves comfortable. You'll all be here for a very long time!"

And the man with the woman's voice laughed again, throwing his head back and howling like a mad dog.

Chapter Nine

"But you look so surprised, my child!" the old blind man said to Erin. "You have not been reading your book as fast as you should, I see! So I will give you and your friends and sister time to read more of it now. Yes, keep reading, my children! Read this book quickly — or there will be a bad end for you, Erin, dear."

He stood and limped across the room straight toward the staircase as if he had eyes. As he walked, he hunched lower and lower, his back sinking into a deep stoop.

As the girls watched, horrified, his gray hair grew longer and his baggy pants changed into a baggy dress.

This couldn't be real! But it was!

When the old man reached the stairway, he whirled about to face his visitors again — and the girls saw that he had transformed himself into the old woman from Harriman's Book Shoppe!

The old woman smiled kindly. She looked at them, and the girls could tell that her eyes worked once again. The smears of mud had disappeared, leaving her face clean.

She raised a bony finger in the air.

The girls screamed and screamed, putting their hands to their faces and yelling with horror. They feared for their sanity and they feared for their lives. They just had witnessed the impossible.

The old woman nodded, her pleasant smile unchanged.

"The world is a mysterious place, my children," she croaked. "Mysterious and strange and often wondrous. We understand very little while we walk on this earth. But all of you are learning something now. You are learning a harsh lesson, my children. Keep reading. Keep reading. Keep reading."

As the old woman climbed the steps, she continued to repeat those two words until she had disappeared: "Keep reading. Keep reading. Keep reading."

The girls heard a heavy door slam at the top of the stairs — and the loud metallic click of two locks being bolted shut.

"We're trapped!" Laurie screamed. "She's locked the door!"

"B-but there *was* no door at the top of the stairs," Kerri said.

For several minutes, the girls sobbed into each other's arms. They were locked inside a jail guarded by some kind of spook or goblin or witch, and there seemed no hope of escape!

Why had they ever come to Harriman's Book Shoppe? Why was this happening to them? What had they done to deserve such a ghastly fate?

All these questions and more echoed off the dirty walls of that small, dark basement room.

Until finally, Erin struggled to regain a bit of her composure.

"Listen, you guys," she said, sniffing back tears. "There's *got* to be something we can do to save ourselves."

"No, there isn't!" Kimberly sobbed. "We're finished! Trapped like four worms inside a fisherman's tackle box."

"No, listen!" Erin said. "I have an idea. Maybe we should do what the old lady told us to do. Uh, I mean the old *man* or ghost or whatever that thing is. Remember what she said over and over? 'Keep reading. Keep reading.' "

"I think you're right, sis," Kerri said. "It hasn't helped our luck to *stop* reading the book. And the warning said you have to read every word anyway — or die! I think we should see what it says in the next chapter."

Reluctantly, the other girls agreed.

They all huddled around the dim light as Erin cracked open the cover of *The Terrible Terror Book*.

The shadows wrapped around their shoulders. Small black bugs crawled over the cold cement floor.

Everyone fought back tears.

Erin began to read aloud — and the words she read shocked them all.

The story of Kerrin and Terri had remained remarkably similar to the real-life events that now swirled around Erin and Kerri and their friends: The two fictional girls had traveled by bus to a nearby city, hoping a faith healer they once met at a county fair could cure their mother's injured shoulder. But they had found the healer's shop abandoned and locked — until the door opened by itself. Kerrin and Terri had entered the dirty storefront nervously.

Once inside, the girls had been kidnapped by the mysterious faith healer, and trapped inside a dark basement cell, *The Terrible Terror Book* said.

The story was so eerie and so horrible that it made the girls shiver. It was so terribly like the very things that were happening to them at this moment!

"I don't get it," Erin said, sounding confused and frightened. "I stopped reading the story. But the bad stuff in the book happened anyway. Only this time, it happened to us *before* I read it in the book."

"Don't you see?" Kerri asked. "Everything in *The Terrible Terror Book* is going to happen to us, Erin! I don't think there's anyway to avoid that now! The same bad stuff is going to happen anyway — whether you read the story or not!"

"I see what you mean," Laurie said. "If you read it right away, this book tells about the *future*. But if you wait long enough to read the story, Erin, it will only tell about the *past*! No matter what you do, though, all of it is going to come true!"

"Huh?" Kimberly said, screwing up her eyebrows. "I'm not sure I understand this yet."

"I think I understand," Erin said. "They mean that this book tells what's going to happen to me and my family and friends. I can't stop anything in this book from happening in real life. But if I read about it *before* it happens, at least I can be prepared for the bad stuff. I guess that's better than being surprised. And now I know for sure that the bad things won't stop — until I *finish* this book!"

"I think I'd rather be surprised by bad things," Laurie said uncertainly.

"Well, I *have* to keep reading this book now!" Erin insisted. "No matter how scared it makes me or how much I want to tear it to shreds! I have to keep reading it."

"Yeah, and I think the faster you read it, the faster you get it all over with," Kerri said. "Remember, even the book told you it was safer to read this story as quickly as possible."

"I — I don't think you should read it!" Kimberly shouted. "It's too dangerous! I think you should throw the book into a dark corner and never open it again!"

"Me, too!" Laurie said. "That book is terrible!"

"No! I've *got* to keep reading!" Erin answered. "We're in the middle of this horrible mess, and somehow I just know that the only way to end it all is to keep reading this book."

The four girls hugged each other and dried each other's tears. Once again they huddled together under the faint light of the basement lamp as Erin turned a page of *The Terrible Terror Book*.

And, holding hands, they faced the terrible, terrible future that now surely awaited them all.

<u>Chapter Ten</u>

"Kerrin and Terri could hear the sound of footsteps outside their basement cell. Someone was coming," The Terrible Terror Book said.

Erin was reading the next chapter as calmly as she could, but her voice trembled with fear.

"Yes, someone was heading toward the door of the basement. Someone who was grunting and sniffing and slobbering to himself as he walked. This certainly didn't sound like the faith healer, Kerrin and Terri thought.

"The door cracked open. And then, step by slow step, the heavy feet of someone unfamiliar to the girls trudged toward the basement. Who could this be, they wondered fearfully. What terrible fate was about to befall them now?

"They found out soon enough! Standing now at the bottom of the basement stairs was a monster — a giant hunchback larger than anyone either girl ever had seen.

"In his right hand he held a gleaming knife! The girls saw five inches of cold steel, pointing right at them!"

Just then, the four girls heard a noise. Someone was coming toward the basement door.

They grabbed each other in terror and shrieked! They knew what to expect next.

The basement locks were unbolted. Then slowly, step by step, heavy feet clomped down the spiral staircase from the abandoned book shop above.

These were not the feet of the old woman — or even of the limping, disgusting old man.

These were the footfalls of a large man — a *very* large man!

They had no time to read another word, no time to learn what the monstrous man did to Kerrin and Terri in the story. The real-life girls had to find someplace to hide from the real-life giant coming after them with a five-inch knife!

Each of them scrambled to separate corners of the tiny room, desperate to find any scrap of cover that might conceal them from the killer.

Erin hid behind the rocking chair. Laurie jumped inside a large cardboard box that rested against the wall. Kimberly rolled herself into a human ball hidden by a vast, dense shadow.

But Kerri could find no place to hide!

She looked wildly from one place to the next, but she found no object big enough and no shadow dark enough to hide her.

The steps continued — *clomp, clomp, clomp* — slowly down to the bottom.

The monster stood in the basement, still just a silhouette in the dim light. But the girls could all see the huge knife gleaming in the huge hand. Light glinted off the blade, at least five inches of razor-sharp steel pointed toward — yes, *directly toward Kerri*!

The giant took a step forward.

Kerri squealed and backed up until she hit the wall at the rear of the basement. She pressed against the wall, trying to get as far away from the beast as she could.

As she did, the wall slid partially open!

It was a false wall — a door that led into a narrow tunnel!

Kerri wasted no time.

"Come on!" she screamed — and ran for her life!

Chapter Eleven

The other girls bolted from their hiding places.

Everyone knew the monster man had only one thing on his mind: murder!

The four friends plunged into the dark tunnel and ran faster than they had ever run before.

"Hurry!" shouted Kimberly, who was last in the line of frantic runners. "He's coming after us! I can hear his footsteps!"

It was true. The footsteps fell fast and heavy — *CLOMP*, *CLOMP*, *CLOMP*, *CLOMP*, *CLOMP*!

They echoed through the black hall, each *clomp* terrifying the girls, and warning any of them who tripped or tired too quickly.

Death was nipping at their heels!

The girls could see little in the blackness, and

they had no idea where they were going. Leading the way, Kerri ran at a gallop, her arms stretched out to protect her face in case she bumped into something.

The others followed her, fixing their eyes on Kerri's tan T-shirt.

At any moment, though, one of them might stumble over something lurking in the darkness — a stick, a stone, anything — and fall into the hands of the monster!

It was a long and bloodcurdling run. All four girls soon felt exhausted.

Still they ran on, groaning and huffing with every step. Despite their fatigue, they ran faster, and faster still, because they could all hear the awful truth: The footsteps behind them were coming faster, clomping louder.

That meant they were getting nearer!

The giant was running faster than the girls, and he was gaining on them quickly!

"Hurry, Kerri!" Erin screamed. "We've got to run faster!"

"I *can't* run any faster!" Kerri hollered.

The tunnel seemed to get narrower as the girls raced along. They scuffed their elbows and scraped their knees as the walls closed in on them. They banged shoulders and hips, they stubbed toes and fingers on walls that felt as if they were made of large rocks.

And they wondered where the tunnel was taking them — or whether it would end suddenly, leaving them trapped in the darkness with a mad killer.

They had no time to do anything but run. The monster was almost near enough to lunge, knife-first, at Kimberly!

As he came closer and closer, the giant began to growl in his fury, like a tiger ready to pounce. He was so close that Kimberly could hear the rattling of his belt buckle. She could actually feel his hot breath against the back of her neck.

It was useless. There was no escape!

She wrapped her arms over her head and screamed!

"Aaaaaaaahh!"

Chapter Twelve

As the monster stabbed wildly in the blackness toward Kimberly, his foot found a pool of water that had dripped down the walls and collected in a hollow of the floor.

He skidded and sailed headfirst toward the rock wall, still growling as he flew through the air.

But as he soared, he also slashed furiously with his steel blade!

And the knife found Kimberly!

She felt the cold metal pierce her skin and sink into her flesh. She felt the warm blood begin to drain from her body.

She wailed like a wounded cat and collapsed. The giant roared, and then slammed into the wall.

He fell to the concrete limp as a rag doll and lay motionless on the floor. Beside him, Kimberly cried and writhed in pain.

When the other girls heard the commotion, they stopped and turned just in time to see the knife plunge into Kimberly and the monster ram into the wall.

They ran back, all screaming at once. "Kimberly! Are you all right? Kim! Say something!"

"I'm hurt!" Kimberly cried. "He stabbed me in the back!"

"Let me look at it!" Erin yelled. "Stand back! I've had first-aid courses."

Erin leaned close and felt the trickle of warm blood bubbling through Kimberly's blouse.

"We need to get her to a doctor!" Erin shouted. "Right away!" Then she turned back to Kimberly. "You're going to be OK," she said. "Honest! The knife didn't get your back. It feels like he just grazed your shoulder. I can't see very well in here, but I can tell it didn't go in very deep. And I'm sure it didn't do much damage. Still, a doctor needs to put some antiseptic on it to kill the germs. You might even need a stitch or two."

"What'll we do for Kimberly in the meantime, sis?" Kerri wondered. "We're stuck in this tunnel and who knows when we'll find our way out? It might be hours before we get her to a doctor."

"We'll have to make a bandage for her," Erin said. "Does anyone have a handkerchief or anything?"

"I do," Laurie said. "Here, Erin."

"Hurry, Erin!" Kerri said. "This monster might come to any minute — and come after us again!"

Within a few moments, Erin had fashioned a triangular bandage out of Laurie's handkerchief. She pulled a barrette from her hair and pushing the metal end through the handkerchief and Kimberly's blouse, turning the barrette into a safety pin to hold the bandage in place.

"There," Erin said. "That should help stop the bleeding."

"Ouch!" Kimberly said. "It really stings, Erin!"

"It'll be all right for a while," Erin said. "Come

on, you guys. We've got to get out of here before this maniac wakes up!"

Erin helped Kimberly stand and steadied her while she regained her balance. Then Kimberly trotted down the tunnel. The other girls followed close behind.

They ran for nearly ten minutes, then stopped to rest, puffing and moaning.

Laurie doubled over, holding her stomach. "I can't run another step," she said.

"Neither can I," Kimberly said. "And my shoulder hurts. I feel really weak."

"Is this tunnel ever going to end?" Kimberly asked. "Where is it going?"

"I wish we could find some way out of here!" Erin exclaimed.

The girls bent over and put their hands on their knees, trying to catch their breath and decide what to do next.

Instead, one by one, they began to cry.

"We're never going to get out of here!" Kerri wailed.

"We're finished!" Erin sobbed.

"It's hopeless!" Kimberly cried.

"I'll never see home again!" Laurie sniffed.

The girls' courage failed them. They surrendered completely to their fears.

They sobbed and ranted against their bad luck. They hugged each other and held hands, four kids confronting a black, terrible death.

Until Kimberly suddenly stopped crying and snapped her fingers.

"Wait! I've got an idea," she said. "The book! *The Terrible Terror Book*! You've still got it, don't you, Erin?"

"Yeah, unfortunately," Erin said. "It's right here in my hand. I almost dropped it while we were running but I held on."

"That's good," Kimberly said, "because we can use the book to figure out how to get away. I'll bet the girls in the book escaped from the monster the same way we did. They must have run into some dark tunnel or something. If we read the book, we can learn how they got out and then just do that same thing!"

"Brilliant!" Kerri said. "For once, the book can *help* us!"

"Yeah, except one thing," Erin said. "We can't see well enough in here to read."

"Oh, yes we can!" Laurie said. "I have a little flashlight on my key chain."

"You're amazing!" Kimberly said. "Do you carry everything in your pockets?"

"Yeah, you should be on Let's Make A Deal or some game show like that," Kerri said.

"All right, cool it," Erin said sternly. "We don't have any time to fool around. That killer still might come after us. Let's start reading."

The four girls collected themselves into a tight ring, shoulder to shoulder in the darkness. Erin shined the flashlight on the pages of *The Terrible Terror Book*.

In the story, Kerrin and Terri had frantically backed away from the monstrous hunchback who held the five-inch knife. They had bumped into a bookcase that really was a door.

Then they had run into the dark corridor that led from their basement cell, with the mad murderer following just behind. Just as the giant was ready to attack Kerrin, he had slipped and knocked himself unconscious, slashing at her back with the blade while he fell. Kerrin's shoulder was cut and bleeding.

Once again, the events in *The Terrible Terror Book* closely resembled the frightening events the real-life girls had survived. The girls still could not believe it.

Erin continued reading aloud, her whispers echoing through the tunnel:

"The sisters knew they hadn't long before the monster hunchback awakened from his knock on the head and resumed his pursuit of them!

"So Terri quickly fashioned a triangular bandage from a handkerchief in her pocket, placing it over Kerrin's wounded shoulder. Then the two girls wasted no time in making another run toward safety — wherever safety might be in such a black and awful place!

"They ran until they felt ready to drop to the concrete floor in total exhaustion. And with no end in

sight, they finally stopped to rest, breaking into tears of sorrow for their hopeless plight. They knew they were doomed.

"The end was near!

"But then Kerrin heard something.

" 'Listen, sis!' she said. 'I hear some noise. It almost sounds like water! Maybe there's an underground pipe we can follow out of here!'

"Fighting off their fatigue, Kerrin and Terri raced toward the distant sound of running water — until their dark path ended abruptly.

"Stretched out before them was a large sewer pipe filled with foul, stinking, brown water. Cockroaches and water beetles and rats swam in it everywhere. And there was nowhere to walk, no possible way to follow the water out to safety — except to jump in and swim in the disgusting stuff.

" 'Ewwww! Gross!' the sisters gagged.

"But at that moment, they heard footsteps bounding down the dark corridor — and they knew that the giant hunchback was on their trail again. They had

*two choices: stay and die, or dive into the sickening
water.*

*" 'Come on, sis! Jump!' Kerrin shouted, leap-
ing feet-first into the sewage."*

"No! I can't do it!" Laurie protested. "That
means there must be a sewer pipe up ahead. I can't
jump into that kind of sewage with all those gross
creatures swimming in it!"

"There's *no* way!" Kimberly said. "I'd rather let
the giant carve me into ribbons!"

Erin began to say something. Then she hesitated,
turning her head to listen.

It was a terrifying sound!

Footsteps!

CLOMP, CLOMP, CLOMP, CLOMP, CLOMP!

"He's coming after us again!" Erin shouted.
"We have to run or that giant will carve us up like a
turkey! Come *on!* We've *got* to make a run for that
sewer!"

Chapter Thirteen

"No! I can't!" Laurie whined. "I'm staying here! I'd rather *die* than jump into a sewer with rats!"

Erin, Kerri and Kimberly were on their feet, ready to run. But they refused to leave their friend behind, even though the clomping footsteps were drawing nearer and nearer.

"Laurie! Come *on*!" Kimberly shouted, tugging on her friend's arm. "We don't have time for this!"

"Get up right now!" Erin commanded. "If you don't, we're *all* going to die! Run, Laurie! He's coming!"

"I *can't*!" Laurie insisted.

"You can!" Kerri shouted.

Angrily, Kerri pushed on Laurie's back as the others yanked on her arms. It worked! Whether she liked it or not, Laurie was suddenly on her feet.

At last her fear of the sewer gave way to her fear of the monster running toward them with a huge knife. Her legs began to move, and finally she broke into a run.

The girls sprinted away from the clomping sound. The clomping behind them grew louder. Suddenly up ahead they heard another sound — the *whoosh* of running water.

It had to be the sewer! Their only route to escape!

They ran on, and soon they saw it in front of them, just as *The Terrible Terror Book* had described it: a brown, filthy sewer filled with rats and beetles and cockroaches. It made them want to throw up.

"Ewwwwww!" they said, all at once. "Gross!"

"I cannot jump into that sewer!" Laurie said emphatically. "I know the monster will get me, but I hate rats and cockroaches! I *hate* them! I can't do it!"

Then the sound echoed again through the tunnel: *CLOMP, CLOMP, CLOMP, CLOMP, CLOMP*!

It wouldn't be long now before the monster man rounded the corner and sprinted toward them holding the blade that had already been stained with Kimberly's blood.

"Come on, Laurie!" Kimberly argued. "If I can do it, you can do it! I hate rats and roaches as much as you do, but we have to save ourselves!"

"Everybody grab someone else's hand," Erin said. "Come on, you guys. Just do it! Take someone's hand!"

Erin held on to *The Terrible Terror Book* tightly with one hand and clasped Kerri's hand with the other. Kerri took Kimberly's hand, and Kimberly took Laurie's hand — and Laurie, with her free hand, held her nose.

"Keep your eyes closed when you land or this dirty water will give you an infection, OK?" Erin said. "Now, when I say 'go,' we all jump! Ready? One! Two! Three — *GO!*"

Together, the four girls leaped into the brown water.

The liquid flowed swiftly through the large

metal sewage system, carrying the girls away from the giant who stood angry and helpless at the water's edge. Apparently, mad as he was, he didn't want to kill them badly enough to jump into *this*.

As they swam with the current, the girls shouted to each other.

"This is so *gross*!" Kimberly yelled. "It stings my shoulder where that crazy guy stabbed me! And all these disgusting creatures!"

"Use your hands to splash the rats and bugs away," Erin shouted. "Keep swimming! This water will take us somewhere. The faster we swim, the faster we can climb out of this gunk!"

"Pew! This really is awful!" Kerri said, coughing. "I think I'm going to get sick!"

But everyone kept moving forward quickly — except Laurie. Laurie just could not handle this foul swim through a sewer pipe as well as the others.

She looked up and saw three enormous gray rats paddling furiously toward her. At the same moment, she felt five or six cockroaches climbing in her hair and on her face.

Instead of picking off the bugs and splashing away the rats, she panicked. She stopped swimming. She just treaded water and screamed.

"I — I can't go on!" she hollered. "I can't take it! I knew the rats would get me! *Heeeelllp*!"

Laurie trailed behind the others, and the water was moving too fast for Erin or Kerri or Kimberly to swim back to help her.

There was nothing anyone could do!

The three big rats, their teeth flashing, were almost on top of Laurie. They looked starved, and Laurie just knew they were going to pounce on her and start chewing on her face.

As Laurie looked into their beady rat eyes, the fear became too much for her — and she passed out! She fell completely unconscious and started to slide under the thick brown water, just as the rats opened their mouths to take their first bites.

Laurie was either about to drown at the bottom of a filthy sewer full of gunk and sludge — or become a rat sandwich!

Chapter Fourteen

"Laurie! Wake *up*!" Erin bellowed, looking back helplessly as her friend sank below the surface. "Wake up, *please*!"

"Please help her!" Kimberly shouted in desperation. "*Aaaaaahh*!"

There seemed to be nothing anyone could do.

But Kerri refused to give up. She grabbed onto a large stick above her that had become jammed in a seam of the sewer pipe. Holding onto it, she resisted the current and waited for Laurie to float downstream toward her.

Just as Laurie fell unconscious, just as the rats closed in for the kill, Kerri reached out frantically for her sister's friend. Laurie was under the surface, and Kerri splashed frantically.

She felt nothing. She feared Laurie had drifted beyond her reach. She groped once more through the murky water, and felt her hands brush against strands of something.

Laurie's hair!

Kerri grabbed a handful of the hair and pulled with all her strength. The swift current pulled at her clothes, almost causing her to lose her grip on the stick. The flowing water yanked Laurie downstream, nearly wrenching her free of Kerri's grasp.

But she pulled and yanked, and finally raised Laurie's head out of the filthy water.

The thrashing and splashing scared away the rats and roaches, which scampered off and were carried away by the current.

Kerri had done it! She stayed calm in a terrible crisis, and she had saved Laurie's life.

"Yes! Yes!" Erin shouted back to her sister. "Hold on to her! You're incredible, sis!"

"Yessssss!" Kimberly screamed. "Hang on, Kerri!"

Kerri felt her grip loosening, but she hung on for dear life, and finally Laurie began to revive. She coughed, spewing water from her mouth, and her eyelids began to flutter.

"Wh-what's happening?" she asked. "You're hurting my hair! Let go!"

Kerri let go of Laurie's hair and grabbed her under her arms.

"Sorry," she said. "It was the only way I could grab you. Are you all right? Can you swim now?"

"I think so," Laurie said. "Stay with me, OK? I don't want to be around any more rats."

"OK, Laurie," Kerri said. "I'm going to let go of you now, and I'll jump in right after. We have to catch up with Erin and Kimberly. Ready?"

Laurie nodded. Kerri released her grip on Laurie, let go of the stick, and plunged back into the flowing muck.

The girls swam feverishly, pushed along by the current. After a minute or so of hard stroking, they caught up with Kimberly and Erin, who had been floating along as slowly as they could manage.

Together, the exhausted girls drifted on and on and on.

The pipe seemed endless. As they floated around each bend, the girls hoped they would see an opening, a way out. Each time, they were disappointed. They could see nothing but more of the long metal tube stretching interminably into the distance.

Paddling just enough to keep their heads above water, the girls raced on through the sewer system.

Finally, over the bubbling of the water, they heard something in the distance. The sound of — what *was* that?

"It's almost like a train roaring somewhere," Erin shouted. "I can't tell what it is!"

"Yeah, or maybe some huge motor," Kerri said, splashing water at a cockroach. "Maybe there's a factory around here. It's loud!"

"Whatever it is, it's getting louder," Kimberly yelled.

"Maybe this sewer will finally empty into some

tank or something and we can get out of this disgusting water!" Laurie said.

The girls strained their eyes, trying to see what lay ahead. They could see only more of the pipe, stretching on and on and on.

Suddenly, out of nowhere, they saw clear blue sky! It winked at them bright and blue — not above them, but right at the end of the pipe.

They glanced at each other worriedly. What did this mean?

As the roaring quickly grew louder and louder, Erin realized what was going on.

"Oh, no!" she shouted. "It's a waterfall! The sewage must go over the top of some kind of dam — and we're going to go over with it!"

"It has to be a huge waterfall!" Kerri yelled. "It's so loud! What can we do? We're goners!"

Before anyone could say another word, the girls found themselves swept forward in a frenzy of filthy water, and flung furiously into the air!

They had been catapulted over the top of an

enormous dam!

They screamed wildly into the wind as they plunged down, down, down, falling faster and faster and faster, like skydivers hurtling toward earth with no parachutes to slow their drop!

Chapter Fifteen

The girls felt as if they had dropped off the end of the earth.

There was nothing below their feet but air. They had nothing to grab on to. They saw nothing to save them from the perilous fall.

They flailed their arms and legs in the wind as they plummeted downward.

Down they fell toward a massive brown lake — sewage water that collected in a huge concrete pool.

The four friends shared just one thought at that instant, just one hope: that the water was deep enough so they could avoid smashing into the bottom of that concrete pool!

If the sewage was deep, they might survive. But

if it was shallow, they would be killed.

They closed their eyes and screamed.

One after another, they splashed into the water, sinking farther and farther below the surface. Then one after another, they all rose to the surface, gasping for breath and coughing and spitting — but happy just to be alive.

The pool had been deep enough after all. Everyone had survived the fearsome plunge over the dam.

"Are you OK?" Erin asked Kerri.

"I'm all right," Kerri answered, gasping after being underwater so long. "Are *you* OK?"

"Yeah," Erin replied, coughing. "Are you guys?"

"I'm OK," Kimberly said. "But my shoulder hurts. I want to get this bandage off."

"I'm fine, but let's get the heck out of this horrible sewage!" Laurie spat.

Several workers at the sewage plant had watched the girls fall into the tank. They rushed to pull the girls from the stinking water.

"How did you girls get into that sewer system?" one of the workers asked. "It's a closed system. There's no way to get inside those pipes."

"Are you girls hurt?" another worker asked. "My gosh, I've never seen anyone fall so far without being injured."

The men showed the girls where they could shower and gave them special soap to clean away the filth of the sewer. Then they handed the girls some old, blue city uniforms to wear.

One worker even found a first-aid kit, putting gobs of antiseptic ointment on Kimberly's wounded shoulder before covering it with a sterile bandage.

Things finally had taken a turn for the better. Maybe, Erin and Kerri thought, their misfortunes were over at last.

The workers said they would drive each of the girls home, making sure they all arrived back with their parents safely.

Erin sighed, and sagged with relief. She sat on a bench and relaxed, letting the tension of the past few hours flow out of her.

She looked around the sewer plan and noticed, in the distance, another worker. He wore a blue city uniform, and he was limping slowly toward them. He was still too far away for Erin to see his face.

But she saw that he was very short, and his shoulders were hunched over.

His hair was gray, and on top of it he wore a red and black bandanna.

"Are you all right, my children?" the man called, his voice sounding like that of a hoarse old woman. "I was worried about you. Come here, my children! Don't be afraid. I want to talk to you!"

Chapter Sixteen

The girls sat frozen with terror. It was impossible!

It was him — or *her*! The ghost or goblin, the witch or spook from Harriman's Book Shoppe!

"*Run!*" Erin screamed.

Despite their shock, the girls ran as if they were propelled by wings.

They flew from the sewage plant, scrambling down the steps and bounding over a low wall like hurdlers in a track meet.

Their fear fueled them with wild energy, and they used every ounce of it to get as far away as possible from the man-woman wearing the red and black bandanna.

When at last their energy was drained, the four

girls stopped along a street somewhere, panting heavily. When they had recovered some of their wind, they wondered aloud what terrible thing would happen to them next and when their nightmare would end.

"There's only one way to find out for sure," Kerri said. "We have to keep reading the book."

Kimberly gasped.

"Oh, no!" she cried. "The book! We must have lost it when we fell over the dam at the sewage plant!"

"And if she can't read it, Erin's going to die for sure!" Laurie said. "This is terrible!"

"We've got to think of some way to find it, you guys," Kerri said. "We *have* to!"

"No, we don't!" Erin said. "I've still got it — right here!"

She pulled the slim volume from under her borrowed shirt. The pages were wet, but still readable.

"I haven't forgotten for a second how important this book is," Erin said. "When I realized we were going over the dam, I stuffed it under my belt. Then I hid the book inside my T-shirt before the workers pulled us

103

out. I rinsed if off in the shower, and now it's fine, though still pretty damp."

"That was great thinking, considering the panic we were in," Laurie said. "Smart work, girl!"

"Thanks," Erin said. "But Kerri's right — we have to keep reading this book. It's the only way to end all the awful things happening to us. Come on, let's find someplace where we can sit down."

The girls, wearing baggy blue work clothes with rolled-up sleeves and pant legs, wandered down the street.

Soon, they found the hulk of a demolished building — just piles of wood and brick scattered around an abandoned yard of tall weeds. They sat down amid the debris, huddling close together as they had done so often during the past day.

After slowly opening *The Terrible Terror Book*, Erin began to read. To no one's surprise, the fictional characters had suffered problems very similar to those of the real-life girls.

In the story, Terri had nearly drowned when she

panicked during an attack by swimming rats. And Kerrin and Terri had survived a fall over a dam, just as Erin and Kerri and Kimberly and Laurie had.

The storybook sisters even were forced to run away from the terrible faith healer once more — the same faith healer who had locked them in the basement cell and sent a monster to kill them with a knife.

It was all so much like the awful events that the four real girls had just endured that their panic almost bubbled to the surface again as they heard the words read aloud.

Now it was time to read more of the terrible story in *The Terrible Terror Book* — time to learn what terrifying things were going to happen next.

Erin looked around, glancing worriedly into each of the girl's eyes. She turned the page and started to read:

"Exhausted after running away from the faith healer again, Kerrin and Terri rested amid the rubble of an abandoned house. At least it was quiet there, Kerrin thought. Maybe all the bad things would end if

they could only rest for a while — and stay away from the strange, dangerous faith healer.

"But the bad things would not end!

"The worst was yet to come!

"For it was not long until a familiar car appeared in the distance, a very familiar car indeed.

"It was the car owned by their mother. The mother who, worried to tears by her daughters' disappearance, had driven everywhere looking for them. Now, through a stroke of luck, she had spotted them sitting in the abandoned building.

"But the good luck soon turned to bad.

"When their mother stopped the car and opened the door to greet them, the family dog, Mustard, darted into the street, barking happily. At that moment, another car passed by from the opposite direction and crashed into the dog!

"The impact threw Mustard twenty feet into the air. He landed hard on the pavement and lay there motionless, without making a sound.

"The string of misfortunes was not over yet for

this frightened family. This time, their faithful little dog, Mustard, was the victim.

"For it was apparent to them all. Mustard was dead!"

Erin slammed the book shut. She could not stand to read another word.

The story seemed so horrible to her — the death of a poor, innocent dog. Why did that have to be part of the plot?

Then she remembered what this story must mean for *her* family, and *her* dog.

Buster!

Oh, no, she thought. Not cute, faithful Buster!

The girls stared at each other, their expressions terrified and helpless. What could they do? How could they stop it from coming true? How could they save Buster's life?

At that instant, they heard the sound of a car approaching. Erin and Kerri recognized it right away. It was their mother's car!

Incredibly, impossibly, she had really found

them. The girls could see that Buster was inside the car with her, jumping around the front seat, eager to greet them.

All four girls jumped to their feet and ran into the street, waving their arms.

"No, Mom!" Erin screamed. "Don't open the door!"

"Mom!" Kerri bellowed. "Stop! Don't get out!"

"No, no, no!" Kimberly and Laurie shouted. "Stop! Wait!"

But it was too late.

The car had already stopped. The driver's door had already opened. Buster was already in the street, barking and wagging his tail.

Erin lunged to grab his collar, but Buster darted happily away — into the middle of the street.

At that moment, she looked up to see another car zooming down the street, bearing down on Buster.

"*Buster*!" they all screamed. "*Buster, run*!"

Chapter Seventeen

But Buster had no chance to run.

The car slammed into him, knocking him high into the air. He landed in a heap and lay motionless in the middle of the street.

Erin and Kerri ran to their dog, sobbing and talking to him and hugging him. It was no use, though. There was nothing they could do.

Buster was dead.

The Terrible Terror Book had killed their dog!

And the girls knew the bad luck was not over yet. They still had several pages of the book left to read. Things were only going to get worse.

Erin and Kerri decided on the ride home that it was time to tell their mother everything.

She *had* to know now. Because now, it seemed,

anything could happen.

The sisters would describe everything that had happened since Kerri bought the book. They would even read their mother parts of the story to prove how the story in the book had predicted their own fate.

At least Kimberly and Laurie were there, too, to help tell the incredible truth about *The Terrible Terror Book*. Their mother would never believe them, anyway, even though her arm was still in a sling from her broken shoulder. But at least four of them would all be telling the same story.

Strangely enough, though, they were wrong. Their mother believed every word they said, right away.

"I *know* you fell off a tall dam, girls," she said. "When you ran away from the plant, one of the workers searched your clothes and found an ID Kerri must have left behind with our phone number. He called me and explained what had happened."

"The rest is true, too, Mom," Erin said.

"It really is," Laurie said.

"I know, girls," their mother said, starting to

cry. "Those passages from the book about falling off the ladder and going over the sewage dam — well, I can tell that this is a very strange, very terrible book, and it has some terrible hold on our family. But I don't know what to do about it. Your father is still away on a business trip. And if I call him and tell him this story, he'll think I've lost my mind."

"But Dad's flying home tonight, Mom," Kerri said. "We'll all tell him about it together."

"Once he looks at this book, he'll *have* to believe us," said Erin.

"Maybe you're right, girls," their mother said. "I *hope* you're right. Maybe your father will know how to break the spell of this awful book!"

Everyone in the car felt scared and sad and tired. All their mother could do was worry about her daughters and their friends. All the girls could do was think about Buster's broken body lying in the trunk.

And all five of them were afraid to read another page of *The Terrible Terror Book*, knowing that whatever happened in the story would happen soon in real life, too.

"But Mom, we've *got* to keep reading!" Erin said finally. "We've already found out that it doesn't help to stop reading the story. The stuff keeps happening. We'll never be done with this nightmare until we finish the book."

"She's right, Mom," Kerri said.

Everyone in the car fell silent. The only sounds were the rumble of the engine and the thumping of the tires over seams in the road.

Her hands trembling, Erin opened *The Terrible Terror Book* again. She began to read the tale of Kerrin and Terri — the tale that was going to tell them all about their own frightening future:

"*Their dog was dead. Nothing, Terri thought, could get any worse now.*

"*She was wrong. Death would visit the family again very soon!*

"*And this time, far more than the life of a dog was at stake!*

"*When the girls arrived home with their*

mother, they all went out to the garden to bury Mustard's body. Then they returned to the house, quietly drinking milk around the kitchen table as they talked about their grief and their fears.

"When the phone rang, the three of them jumped. Their mother hurried to answer it.

"She listened intently for a moment. Then her face contorted into an expression of horror, shock and sorrow.

" 'No, it can't be!' she said. 'Are you sure? You know for sure it was him?'

"She hung up the phone, collapsed at the kitchen table, and began to sob.

" 'Mom!' the girls pleaded. 'What's wrong? Tell us!'

"After a moment, the mother looked into her daughters' eyes, grabbed each of them around the shoulders and hugged them tightly.

" 'Girls, I'm so sorry to tell you this,' she said. 'It's terrible news! It's about your father. That was the airline calling. He was a passenger on a plane that crashed this afternoon. He's dead!' "

Chapter Eighteen

The real-life mother nearly drove off the road when she heard those words!

And she wasn't the only one who was shocked. Everyone in the car was in a total panic.

None of them could talk. None of them could think. None of them could even breathe.

Their mother drove like a wild woman, speeding toward home, tears streaming down her face. Erin and Kerri cried, too, tears flowing down their cheeks and spattering onto their borrowed blue uniforms.

Not my father, Erin thought. Please make it stop! Make this terrible book stop tormenting everyone!

And please, *please* let my wonderful father come home safely!

Erin was furious at *The Terrible Terror Book*.

She wanted to tear it into pieces and scatter the shreds out the car window. But she believed that the bad luck would never end until she had read the last word on the last page.

Their mother, terrified, drove faster and faster. The car screeched around corners on two wheels.

"Mom!" Kerri cried. "Slow down!"

"I have to get home, right away," their mother sobbed. "In our bedroom, I have the number where I can call your father. I have to tell him not to take that plane! He has to take a train or a bus or a car — anything but a plane!"

The family car squealed around another corner and skidded to a stop in the driveway. Their mother threw open the door, sprinted up the steps of their home and disappeared inside.

The girls raced up the steps behind her.

But the next instant, they heard a scream from the kitchen!

A scream — and then a shout!

What had happened. Was there already terrible

news about a plane crash?

The girls ran into the kitchen only to find the mother crying — and hugging her husband with her one good arm.

Their father was home early, safe and sound.

He hadn't died in a plane crash after all!

"Oh, I love you!" their mother was saying. "I love you!"

"Daddy!" Erin and Kerri shouted. "You're all right!" They ran to hug him.

"I've only been away three days," their father said. "What a homecoming! My meeting this morning was shorter than I expected, so I caught an earlier flight. Why is everybody crying?"

After a few moments, they gathered around the kitchen table, snacking on sandwiches and milk as Erin and Kerri and Kimberly and Laurie retold their strange, frightening tale.

The father looked bewildered.

He listened to the long account of misery, and heard about one misadventure after another. The girls read to him from *The Terrible Terror Book*. For nearly two hours, he heard the stories and asked questions — and still refused to believe a word of it.

At last, he listened to his wife telling him about the call from the sewage worker. He grabbed the book, thumbed through it, and read that chapter of the book for himself.

The stories matched. What had happened in the book was almost identical to what the sewage worker had told his wife. And his children were wearing blue city uniforms.

Finally, even this skeptical businessman became convinced of the book's mysterious curse.

He stared down at the volume with dread.

"I think it's clear what we have to do," he said, his voice hoarse and a little uncertain. "Erin has to finish reading this book to all of us. Right now! These problems won't end until the book is done."

"I agree, Daddy," Erin said. "I have to finish the book. Besides, one good thing is that what just happened in the story didn't come true for us! There was no plane crash! Maybe the curse is over."

"Maybe," Kerri said. "Or maybe *not!*"

Slowly, Erin opened the pages of the book and began to read aloud:

"The girls and their mother cried for several long minutes together. A dear father, a dear husband was dead.

"Just then the phone rang. Their mother gathered enough strength to answer. Again she listened intently. But this time, she broke into a grin. Tears of joy streaked down her cheeks.

" 'You're absolutely sure? Oh, thank you so much!' she said, hanging up the phone. 'He's alive, girls! Your father and everyone on that plane is fine! It didn't even crash! It was all a scare caused by a strange radar and radio malfunction. The airport thought the plane went down — but it really didn't! Your father will be home for dinner!'

"And with those words, the family's long and frightening spell of bad luck came at last to an end.

"The father arrived home safely to the tearful

embrace of his wife and children. The injuries to the mother's back and shoulder soon healed, as did Kerrin's wound from the knife. And Kerrin and Terri never again saw the strange faith healer who had brought them so much trouble and terror.

"And if, dear reader, you have reached this point in The Terrible Terror Book, *your string of mishaps and misfortunes is also over, as well."*

Was it true? Was it really over?

Yes, it must be true, they all agreed. The spell was broken!

Erin and Kerri hugged each other. Kimberly and Laurie exchanged high fives. Everyone in the room smiled and sighed with relief.

"That's so great," Laurie said with a grin. "But I don't get it. Why did any of this happen? What's the deal with this book anyway? It was so weird, the way this old story really seemed to be about Erin and Kerri — and the way it made awful stuff happen to all of us."

"I don't know, Laurie," Erin said. "I don't get it either. I just know I'd better keep reading the story now. We've still got a little left to finish, and I want to make sure I don't miss even a single word. Then we can burn this book and be done with it forever!"

Erin turned the page and continued to read. Her parents, her sister, and her friends leaned forward with rapt attention:

"You, dear Erin, have been tested — and you have proven yourself courageous and strong. Perhaps far more courageous and far stronger than you ever imagined yourself to be. And all your troubles have helped your sister and your friends find more of their own courage and strength, as well.

"This book contains a lesson, you see — a hard lesson which few are lucky enough to learn. You were chosen to discover that lesson through this book, which was prepared long ago just for you!

"There are no answers for many of the questions you have about The Terrible Terror Book. *You will never discover this volume's great mysteries. Some mysteries in life are not meant to be solved.*

"But know this much and remember it always:

"Fear is the worst disease that afflicts mankind,

"It can cripple your body and cripple your mind —

"But if you persevere, push ahead through your pain,

"You'll be amazed at the things you will gain.

"We must all go on through darkness and through tears,

"Then the darkness will lift and wash away our fears."

Erin turned the last page and closed the book. Those were *The Terrible Terror Book*'s final words.

Erin wasted no time. She went to the fireplace and burned the book at once.

It was too dangerous, she knew, to keep the book in her library. The story had caused everyone so much suffering. Now that she had finished it, the book had to be destroyed.

But she would never forget the poem that concluded the book. And she would feel forever grateful for the difficult lesson she had learned. Never again would she give in to her fears.

Of course, Erin never again went hunting for the most frightening horror book in the world, either. She had found that once — and once was most certainly enough.

"Hey, sis!" Kerri asked her sometimes with a smile. "Want to read a scary story?"

Whenever Kerri said this, the two sisters laughed and hugged each other and forgot about any silly arguments they'd had.

"Just remember," Erin often answered, "whenever I ask you to get me a scary book, just buy me something in the Shivers collection, OK? That's plenty scary enough for me!"

BE SURE TO READ THESE OTHER
COLD, CLAMMY SHIVERS BOOKS.

THE HAUNTING HOUSE

WHEN CAITLIN MOVES INTO AN OLD
HOUSE, SHE HAS A STRANGE FEELING
SHE IS DISTURBING THE HOUSE'S PEACE.
SHE IS BOTHERED BY STRANGE NOISES.
WEIRD THINGS START TO HAPPEN.
THINGS THAT CANNOT BE EXPLAINED. AT
FIRST CAITLIN THINKS THE HOUSE MAY
BE HAUNTED. BUT SHE SOON STARTS TO
WONDER IF THERE IS SOMETHING AT
WORK EVEN MORE FRIGHTENING THAN
GHOSTS – AND MORE DANGEROUS. ALL
SHE KNOWS FOR SURE IS THIS: SOME
FRIGHTENING PRESENCE IN HER NEW
HOME IS ALSO DEADLY.